PONY TA

MW00945368

LULU AND PEBBLES

— WB —
WAMAN BOOKS

LULU AND PEBBLES

WAMAN BOOKS PUBLISHING

www.luluandpebbles.com

ISBN: 978-1-7357740-7-7 (paperback)
        978-1-7357740-8-4 (epub)

Library of Congress Control Number: 2022905840

Author: Reena Korde Pagnoni
Illustrator: Jon Davis
Editor: Lor Bingham, Calico Editing
Publishing and Design Services: MelindaMartin.me

Publication Date: June 7, 2022

PONY TALES ON THE FARM

LULU AND PEBBLES

Written by Reena Korde Pagnoni
Illustrated by Jon Davis

—— WB ——
WAMAN BOOKS

To Stellario
without whom this book
would not have been written

CONTENTS

1

I WANT A UNICORN

I woke up early, I had bubbles of excitement in my belly. Something amazing was going to happen! Want to know how I knew? Because... it was my birthday, and I was turning eight years old. For the last few years all I'd wished for was a unicorn. I'd wished for one every birthday and every Christmas, and the fact that I hadn't gotten one yet made me wonder if Santa had received any of my letters or if my parents were even listening. Anyway, I had a feeling that today my wish would come true. Really! Here's why I thought that. . .

Daddy grew up on a farm and always said he would be back one day, and guess what? Just four years ago we moved to the farm! I loved it right away, but I think it was more of an adjustment for Mama who was less than thrilled with the idea. "That rooster is so loud!" Mama complained. At first, she was NOT a fan of our rooster, Henry, but over time she grew to love him. . . well okay, maybe not love, but certainly *like* him.

I'd been working hard to show my parents how VERY responsible I was. Well. . . sometimes I forgot to brush my teeth or close the front door but. . . I always remembered to feed our dog, Mr. Buttons, and I knew I would never forget to take care of

Pebbles. Who's Pebbles? My unicorn of course! Yes, I'd already named her!

Living on a farm meant there were always lots of chores to be done so I kind of became responsible whether I wanted to or not. "Feeding the animals and cleaning up after them is not a lot of work, young lady!" Mama would scold anytime I complained.

Sometimes I helped Daddy by feeding the animals—a goat, a rooster and 10 chickens—in addition to feeding Mr. Buttons who basically thought he was one of the farm animals. You would never have known that the silly dog lived in the house because he was always out in the barn with the other animals!

The barn was the MOST fun place on the farm, if you asked me! My brother, Max, and I loved playing hide-and-seek in there. I loved Max. . . but he could be a little twerp at times, like when he cried because he couldn't find me and then I got in trouble for being good at the game!

"Lucia, you know Max is only four years old, for heaven's sake, can't you find an easier hiding spot?" When Mama used my real first name, instead of calling me Lulu, I knew she meant business.

Anyway, last night at dinner I reminded my parents and brother how responsible I was and how much I wanted a unicorn and how INCREDIBLY sad it would be if I didn't get one.

"I am very responsible," I told my parents, "I'm done with all of my spelling homework for the whole entire week and it's only Thursday!"

"That is VERY responsible, and you know what I always say—responsibility doesn't take a day off!" Mama said with a smile.

"Not to mention all the chores I do around the farm," I added for some brownie points.

I noticed my parents exchange a look. What was that look?

After dinner, Mama tucked Max and I into our beds, but I couldn't fall asleep. As I snuggled my stuffed hippo—Stinky—in bed, I couldn't stop thinking about that 'look'. Did that look mean, 'she's getting a unicorn, she's going to be so excited'? or was it one that meant, 'she's going to be so disappointed tomorrow'? Grown-ups can be hard to read sometimes. My best friend, Emma, said that parents have a secret language and they can say everything they need to with an exchange of a look! I wondered where they learned that?!

Maybe it was the 'look' that caused little bubbles to start up in my belly. As I drifted off to sleep, I told myself that 'look' must have meant that when I went downstairs in the morning, there would be a unicorn waiting for me. . .

2

HAPPY BIRTHDAY TO ME!

My eyes popped open when I heard Henry cock-a-doodle-doo'ing in the morning. I couldn't wait to get downstairs, convinced that my unicorn was just standing around waiting for me. I jumped out of bed, screaming "HAPPY BIRTHDAY TO ME!! Today's the day!" Can you imagine my utter surprise when I realized my family wasn't already up and standing outside my room waiting to sing "Happy Birthday" to me? I marched right into my parents' room. I first woke up Mama and Daddy then Max. Even though he could be a real cranky disaster in the mornings, I felt it was only right for Max to celebrate me today too!

I brushed my teeth (not because I wanted to but because I was trying to prove to Mama and Daddy how responsible I was) and ran downstairs. Another not-so-great surprise—no Pebbles! But wait. . . on the table I saw a few presents: three big boxes and one little box with a card that said: *Open Last.* I was a little disappointed that all of the boxes were too small to hold a unicorn, but presents are presents and when they were for me, who was I to turn them away?!

"Happy Birthday, Lulu!" Mama said as she laid one of her big Mama kisses on me.

"Thanks, Mama," I politely responded, trying my best not to make a face.

I wasted no time ripping through my presents. I ripped the first box open. . . new boots. I guessed my old boots were getting small, so although not an exciting present, I'd keep them. Next, I opened the second box. . . three unicorn brushes. . . my heart started beating a little faster. Next, inside the third box I found a rope. . . wait a minute, that wasn't a rope, it was a harness. . . perhaps for a unicorn?! The wheels in my brain started working harder. My heart raced even faster. . . Maybe my parents had somehow shoved a baby unicorn in that little box. I looked up at Daddy with big, hopeful eyes, but he didn't say a word, he just pointed to the last little box.

"Open it, open it!" Max screamed, his excitement boiling over.

This was the lightest of the boxes. I opened it quickly and found a brochure with a picture of a pony on it. I read the big letters on the front of the brochure: *Penny's Pony Rescue*. I looked at Daddy, a little confused.

"Is my unicorn at the pony farm or am I getting riding lessons?" I asked.

"Neither!" he responded. "You're getting what you've always wished for. . . well kinda. . . you're getting a pony!"

I could hardly believe my ears. . . did he just say what I thought he said? "A pony. . . A PONY. . . A POONY!! Like a real life one that's all mine?" My mind wasn't processing any of the words coming out of my mouth. I was so excited I was surprised I didn't jump right out of my jammies. I didn't even care that I didn't get a unicorn. A pony was MUCH better anyway! To be honest (and Mama says you should always be honest), I was worried about getting a unicorn when my best friend, Emma, didn't have one. Emma might have gotten jealous and then we could have gotten into a big fight and not been friends anymore. But Emma had never mentioned wanting a pony. So, now I could keep my best friend AND have my very own pony.

Max was excited too. "A pony, oh boy, we are getting a pony!" he squealed.

"Uh-hum... correction, you little twerp, I'M getting a pony," I corrected him quickly so he didn't get any wrong ideas. "Max, you are a very, very lucky little boy," I informed him. "Not only will you get to stuff your little face with chocolate cake today... but you also get to watch me be responsible with my new pony—Pebbles!"

Max squealed again. "Pebbles... Oh boy, I love that name!"

After breakfast, I ran upstairs to get dressed in my best clothes. *First impressions are very important, and I need to look perfect for the very first time Pebbles sets her eyes on me.* Suddenly, the phone rang, interrupting my thoughts. It was Emma.

"Happy Birthday, Lulu! I can't wait to see you later!"

With all the excitement that had taken place that morning, the thought of seeing

Emma later seemed like the cherry on top of my birthday. It had always been our tradition; we celebrated our birthdays having cake together and a sleepover.

"Thanks, Em, I can't wait to see you either!" I replied.

"I would never miss seeing my best friend on her birthday. . . or your Mama's chocolate cake!" We both laughed. Mama's cake was the best! Just ask Max, who shoveled cake in his mouth with his hands because he claimed it smelled too good to wait for a fork. You couldn't take that kid anywhere; he was such an embarrassment!

"Em, you're never going to believe what I'm getting for my birthday. . ." I started to tell Emma about my pony, but then I stopped. Maybe I'd surprise her when she came over later.

"Well. . . what is it?" Emma asked impatiently.

"It's a surprise, you'll just have to wait until this afternoon," I replied, trying not to burst with excitement.

When I got off the phone with Emma, I quickly made a "Welcome Home" sign for Pebbles. Then ran out to the barn to hang it on the stable door. The only thing missing was my pony.

I can't wait to go pick up Pebbles and bring her home! I thought, gazing at the stable. *Having my own pony is going to be great! This morning I had no idea I even wanted a pony, now it's all I can think about!*

As excitement radiated through my bones, I had no way of knowing that the next few weeks would be far from what I had imagined. . . and that sometimes things don't go as expected…

3

I DON'T THINK SHE LIKES ME!

My parents and I were already by the car ready to go—as usual we were waiting on Max, who was busy hugging Mr. Buttons and saying goodbye. Max acted like he would never see Mr. Buttons again every time we left the farm.

Suddenly, we heard Max's little voice, "Daddy, Mama, come quick—it's Blu!"

Blu was our little goat. Max had named her Blu because, unlike the other goats we had seen, she had one brown eye and. . . one blue eye! Daddy always said: "Goats are very curious and independent animals!" Mama always said: "Blu's curiosity usually gets her into some sort of mischief." I thought she was just playful and nosey.

We went to see what Blu had got up to this time. . . she had somehow gotten her head stuck in the chicken coop! She was *always* up to something. The chickens were clucking away at her head trying to get her out of there. Daddy went over and freed the silly goat before walking back to the car.

"Can we go now?" I said impatiently.

And we were finally on our way!

Penny's Pony Rescue was an hour from our house. I spent most of the car ride looking out the window imagining all the adventures that Pebbles and I would have together. This was going to be the best day ever and no one could ruin it, not even that little twerp whining about why Mr. Buttons couldn't come with us.

"Mama, what *is* a pony rescue?" I asked, trying to distract my mind from the long ride.

"It's a place, well a ranch really, which takes in ponies that need to be cared for because they might have been injured, ill or not properly cared for," Mama explained. "Penny's Pony Rescue has mainly got ponies in it, although they do take in some other animals too."

"And what about my pony? What happened to her?" I asked, hoping that she didn't have a sad story.

"I'm not sure, but we will give her the best home possible with lots of love," Mama replied.

The thought of giving a pony a better life warmed my heart instantly. "I will make sure I love her so much that it makes up for any sadness she's had before she comes to our farm! When I see my Pebbles, I'll give her the biggest hug ever and she will know how much I love her and that I will always be here for her."

"Me too, me too! I'll love the pony too!" Max yelled. He had been so quiet for the past few minutes that I had forgotten he was still in the car!

"You'll need to be careful how you interact with the pony, kids. Horses and ponies can sense human emotions." Daddy added, "She may be a little shy at first, it's important to be calm and gentle around her, no loud noises. She will need time to build trust, then, and only then, can a beautiful friendship form."

The only word I heard from Daddy was 'calm.' Calm? How could I be calm? I took some deep breaths. But seriously, I was about to get a pony and these people wanted me to be calm?!

When we arrived at Penny's Pony Rescue, Miss Penny herself was standing at the gate as though she'd been waiting for us.

She was a nice old lady with crooked teeth. Miss Penny walked us around her rescue center and told us a little about the ponies on the ranch. As we walked, Mama and Daddy periodically interjected with facts about how to properly care for a pony and what they needed every day to live happy, healthy lives. I was impressed with how much homework they had done on ponies. Clearly, getting a pony wasn't a decision they had made that morning. I realized this must have been a carefully considered plan, despite the fact they had sprung it on me that morning. Miss Penny politely agreed with all their facts and pointed out the most important thing was to have love and patience. Her kindness towards the animals made me like her even more.

When we finally got to the stables, Miss Penny told us about a 6-year-old female Shetland pony who had been found on an abandoned farm.

"No one knows what happened to the

family who lived there. I've had her here for a little while and looked after her. I've named her Buttercup. You can change her name if you like," Miss Penny explained.

It was a good thing she said that because I had the perfect name already picked out. Before I could say a word, Max blurted out: "Lulu said the pony's name is Pebbles. . . like rocks. . . but pebbles!"

Miss Penny chuckled at Max's excitement, gave him a gentle tap on his head, and told him that was a wonderful name.

My first impression of Pebbles was not at all as I had expected. She looked sad and broken. Not physically broken like missing feet or anything, but broken like she needed some love and a friend. . . and I knew the perfect person who could give her both—ME!

Pebbles was short and plump, and was brown with disheveled white-ish blond hair. Most people may not think she was the most attractive pony, but to me she was

beautiful and perfect and I fell in love with her immediately. Max didn't know what to make of her. Pebbles clearly did not look like the pony his little mind had imagined.

I couldn't wait another moment to meet my Pebbles. I had forgotten what Daddy had said in the car, about using a soft voice and staying calm. Apparently, that was very good advice and I should have followed it. . . Instead, I ran over to my pony with my arms wide open, ready to plant a big ol' Mama hug on her.

"Hi, Pebbles! I'm Lucia, but you can call me Lulu! I'm going to be your best friend and take good care of you and love you so, so, so much! You're coming home with us; we're going to have so much fun together. . ." The words flooded out of my mouth uncontrollably. "Oh my goodness, you're just so cute and perfect, I love you to pieces." My heart had clearly taken over at this point because I had no control of my mouth.

Pebbles looked right at me, but not with loving, endearing eyes as I had expected, she looked frightened. She slowly backed away from me and moved to the back of the stable. I stopped dead in my tracks and put my hands over my mouth before any more words came flying out and scared Pebbles even more. *Oh no, have I messed everything up? Does Pebbles not like me?* I was disappointed and a little confused by Pebbles' reaction. I didn't want to believe that the pony—my pony—didn't feel the same 'love at first sight' for me that I had for her. I guessed she didn't know that I just wanted to be her friend and love her.

I felt like I was balloon that had been blown up all morning and someone had just taken a needle to it and made it pop! I felt sad and deflated, not to mention a little embarrassed.

"I don't think she likes me!" I said to Mama, fighting back tears. Seeing how upset I was, Mama couldn't hide her disappointment either. She gave me one of her magical hugs that usually made everything better. . . but it didn't work.

"Lulu, sweetie, it's not that the pony doesn't like you, she just doesn't know you yet, that's all," Daddy explained.

Miss Penny agreed, "Honey, the pony just needs time to build trust with you and build a bond. That can take some time, but she'll come around. You just have to be patient with. . . what did you call her? Tebbles?" She turned to Max as she asked.

"Pebbles," I corrected, feeling annoyed that she had already forgotten her name. Max just stood there in silence, taking in everything that was going on. The fact that even the little twerp was able to follow Daddy's advice made me even more frustrated.

A short while later, we loaded up Pebbles in the trailer and headed home. I couldn't have imaged how differently I would feel on the car ride home than I had that morning.

I thought I would be the happiest girl in all the land, having the best birthday ever. Instead, I felt like I'd made an awful first impression with Pebbles and, because of that, she was probably petrified of me. *I really wish I'd listened to Daddy's advice. My energy is too much for poor little Pebbles and my voice is too loud. Now I can't make a second first impression! Why didn't I just stay calm?*

Suddenly, I realized that my disappointment wasn't in Pebbles at all, it was in me…

4

THE UNEXPECTED

When we pulled onto our farm, Daddy started unloading Pebbles from the trailer. Mr. Buttons came over to see what all the commotion was—nothing happened on the farm without Mr. Buttons knowing about it. I noticed that Pebbles was curious about the dog and didn't seem afraid by his approach. Mr. Buttons calmly and

methodically allowed his nose to investigate all the new smells surrounding Pebbles. After a few sniffs, he must have decided that Pebbles was harmless and that she could stay, because he went on his way to see what the chickens were up to.

I was just happy to be home. I ran up to my room, feeling discouraged. I grabbed Stinky—my favorite stuffed animal hippo who always made me feel better—and held him tight. How could one morning be filled with so much disappointment *and* excitement?! This wasn't the birthday I had hoped for. I was emotionally exhausted—and it was only noon.

"Lulu, where are you? Let's play with the pony!" I could hear Max's bubbly little voice throughout the house as he looked for me. A few minutes later, the little twerp found me.

"Max, I'm glad you're here. We need to talk, have a seat," I instructed, pointing to my bed.

Max didn't argue, he climbed up on my bed as he was told.

"What do you think of our pony?" I started questioning slowly, not knowing exactly where I was going with this.

"I love the pony and I love her name!" Max exclaimed. "And she looks funny!"

"It is a great name," I agreed. "But forget about the name for a minute. Do you think we got the right pony?" As soon as the question popped out of my mouth, I was filled with guilt and regret for asking. Although I couldn't help but question it; I couldn't wrap my mind around Pebbles not loving me at first sight. Max looked confused by my question.

I don't know if it was the guilt or Max's look, however, something inside me became clear. I loved Pebbles even if she didn't love me. I was determined to show Pebbles that I loved her no matter how mangled she looked or felt inside or out, or how afraid of me she was. To me she was perfect, and I loved her more than all the unicorns in the world. Of course she was the right pony; she was *my* pony!

As my thoughts became clear, I dismissed Max. "Never mind, Max, you can go now. You've been very helpful, thank you." Max hopped off my bed, shrugged his shoulders and went back outside.

I decided to gather a few things that may comfort Pebbles on her first day in her new home. "Stinky, I think Pebbles needs you more than I do right now so you're moving into the barn for a while, my friend." I gave Stinky one last hug, then reached for the super-soft unicorn blanket off my bed—in case Pebbles got cold at night.

A thought crossed my mind—how would I show Mama and Daddy how responsible I was and take care of my Pebbles if she wouldn't even let me near her? This would have to be a problem for another day, I quickly pushed the thought aside and headed out. Before I could leave my room, something outside my window caught my eye. Something so unexpected that I just stood there watching, unable to move. And that's when I saw it happen…

5

NOT SO TRUE TRUTH

I couldn't believe my eyes! Pebbles was just outside the barn, but she wasn't alone. Our little goat, Blu, must have spotted Pebbles and jumped over to say hello. The amazing thing I couldn't believe was that Pebbles had allowed Blu to get close to her because, unlike Mr. Buttons, Blu was full of energy—just like me! Yet Pebbles hadn't backed away from Blu! In fact, she seemed to like the silly goat. I felt a pinch of jealousy go through my bones. How could I be jealous of a goat? The thought was as ridiculous as something Max would say, so I quickly pushed it aside and kept watching. After a few minutes together, Pebbles started following Blu around the farm. I couldn't believe it. Was this the same little frightened pony? For whatever reason, I guessed Pebbles had trusted the little goat and made her first friend on the farm.

After watching the two animals together for a while, I realized my jealousy had turned into relief. Relief for Pebbles. For the first time in hours, my face and heart were both smiling. I was happy to think of Pebbles feeling more comfortable—even if it was with a silly goat. *This means that Pebbles is able to make friends! Daddy is right, she just needs time to get used to us.* My new revelation gave me hope that one day Pebbles would allow me to get close to her too. And just like that, I was once again lost in a daydream about the many adventures Pebbles and I would have together as best friends.

The phone rang and brought me back to reality.

"Hi, Lulu, I can be over an in hour, does that work? I can't wait to see your big birthday surprise!" It was Emma. Oh no. . . Emma! I had been so focused on how to make Pebbles my friend, that I had completely forgotten about my *actual* friend. I felt a streak of panic go through my body. I certainly couldn't let Emma know what happened at Penny's Pony Rescue that morning or that Pebbles didn't like me. . . yet. And I didn't know how Pebbles would react to Emma. Would she back away from her too? Would Emma think she was weird and unfriendly if she did? I didn't want Emma to not like Pebbles. What a mess! I didn't know what to do. I fumbled with the phone in my hand.

"Hey, Em, um. . . actually I'm not sure we can hang out today after all," I said as the guilt built up in my throat.

"What?! Oh no, why?" Emma's voice sounded utterly disappointed. Hearing it made me feel even worse than I was already feeling.

"Well. . . I'm not feeling that great and I don't want to get you sick." I felt terrible lying to my best friend. . . but I just couldn't deal with yet another disappointment that day of Emma not liking Pebbles or the embarrassment of my very own pony not liking me!

"Not feeling well on your birthday. . . I'm so sorry. I wish there was something I could do for you." Emma's kindness made me want to ball up under the covers and not come out until tomorrow. The truth was, I had wanted to spend my birthday with my best friend eating Mama's chocolate cake like we always did. And I'd wanted to introduce her to my new pony. . . I'd hoped

Emma would love Pebbles just as much as I did. . . but Pebbles had changed all that, and now my day was moving in quite a different direction. In that moment I felt a bit of resentment towards Pebbles for ruining my birthday. The sudden shift in emotions made those bubbles in my belly start up again. I quickly ended the call. "Thanks, Em, I'll call you later, okay? Bye." I could feel the anxiety building as I thought about what would happen if Emma found out I wasn't really sick. I told myself that as long as Emma's parents didn't call my parents to ask how I was feeling, no one would know and everything would be fine. I quickly pushed the thought out of my mind. I was still holding Stinky and the unicorn blanket in my arms. I took a few deep breaths and went outside.

When I got outside, Pebbles and Blu were still together.

"Look, Lulu, Pebbles made a friend," Daddy said with a big smile on his face.

"I think Penny was right, this little pony will come around, she just needs some time."

"You mean she needs time for ME!" I snapped. "She seemed to like Blu right away." The words, wrapped tightly in emotion, just flew out of my mouth. I was happy that Pebbles had made a friend. I just wanted her to like me too!

"Because they are both herd animals, ponies and goats can bond quickly with each other. And they make great barn buddies!" Daddy loved to share his farm knowledge.

I watched the two animals interact for a bit longer while figuring out how to approach Pebbles again. This time I tried to stay as calm as possible, but I was worried she could still feel my nervous energy.

"Hi, Pebbles," I said from afar. "I'm not going to hurt you, I promise. I just want to be your friend, sweet girl," I said in my calmest voice. "Look, I brought you Stinky and a blanket for your first night here." I put my hands out as if Pebbles would reach out and grab them. This time Pebbles didn't move away from me, but she still looked wary of me as if her guard was still up.

I took a deep breath and took a step closer. . . then a little closer. . . a few more steps. . . until I was close enough to touch her. I felt those bubbles again in my belly. They weren't the excitement type of bubbles; they were the nervous type. As I leaned in to pet Pebbles, I felt the bubbles spill over. She must have felt them too because she took a step back. That dreaded step! Sadness fell over me, not only for me but for Pebbles too—just thinking of what kind of sad past she may have had that made her so scared of people. Could that be why she was so afraid? Her past? I didn't know what to do. Before I could do anything at all, I heard a car pull up to the house. Who could that be? Then the worst thing that could have happened just happened! I saw Emma getting out of the car…

6

SURPRISE VISITOR

Oh no, what is she doing here?! I told her I was sick, why is she here? Panicked thoughts filled my head and I totally froze. *What will happen if Emma sees me and knows I'm not really sick?* I couldn't stand the thought of both Pebbles AND Emma being upset with me. The situation could not have gotten any worse. *What if Emma asks how*

I'm doing? Or if Dr. Burns wants to see me? I know he's a vet, but you know how doctors are, when they hear of a sick patient, they are always ready to assist! Now I understand why Mama always says you should never lie.

The second my feet started moving, I quickly ran back inside the house before Emma saw me. I ran as fast as I could up the stairs and into my room, slamming the door shut behind me. I watched from the window as Emma and her father, Dr. Burns, walked over to Daddy. Emma had a blue birthday bag in her hand. She set the bag gently on the floor by the barn and headed over toward Pebbles in awe. Oh no, oh no. . . my heart started racing. I could only image the conversation that Emma, Dr. Burns and Daddy were having. . . Daddy telling Emma that I got a pony for my birthday. I hoped he left out the part of Pebbles not liking me. And what if Emma asked about me? Daddy could tell her I wasn't sick and Emma would be furious with me for lying to her. Not to mention Daddy—he would be mad at me for lying as well.

I watched closely as Emma took a step closer to Pebbles. If she allowed Emma to pet her, then I would know for sure that it was me that Pebbles didn't like. Max came running into my room.

"Lulu, Lulu, Emma's here!" he announced.

"Shhhh. . ." I told Max, realizing my window was slightly open and Emma could probably hear him. I looked outside and saw Emma staring up at my window. She must have seen me because she gave a little wave. Realizing she had seen me, I panicked and quickly ducked, pulling Max down with me. "You little twerp. . . now look what you've done!" I scolded Max in a loud whisper.

"Why are we getting down?" Max asked.

"Because. . . I don't want Emma to see me!" I replied.

"Why not?" Max asked again.

"Just because, now go. . . and if you see Emma, tell her I'm sick!"

"But you're not sick," Max argued. "And Mama said you should never lie!"

I shood Max away and he left. I stayed on the ground for another moment and tried to collect my thoughts. My mind was racing. *Why didn't I just wave back?! I probably looked super suspicious not waving. Emma is probably wondering what's going on. What if she knows that I didn't tell her the truth?*

I slowly peeked my head up and looked back out the window. . . but it was too late; Emma and her dad had already walked back to the car. Great!! Now I'd never know if Pebbles allowed Emma to pet her or not, and I wouldn't know if Emma was mad at me for not waving back.

I waited until Emma's car backed out of the driveway before I went outside. Daddy had brought Pebbles into the stable.

"Lulu. . ." Daddy started, "Emma told

me you weren't feeling well. . ."

"Oh right. . . about that. . ." I felt those nervous bubbles in my belly. Then something totally unexpected happened; to my surprise, Daddy stopped me from continuing.

"No need to explain. . . I had a feeling it had something to do with your pony. When Emma asked me how you were feeling, I just said she's felt better." Technically Daddy wasn't lying because I *had* felt better.

"Thanks, Daddy!" I said as I gave him a big hug, relieved that he'd spared me the embarrassment of having to explain myself. I was so relieved that I forgot to ask him how Pebbles did with Emma. Maybe I didn't want to know!

"Now, young lady, this pony is your responsibility, don't forget to feed her, brush her when she lets you, and give her lots of love," Daddy said as he walked out of the barn. I nodded and felt the weight of the world wash off my shoulders. "Now, say goodnight and come on in for some cake before I eat it all!" Daddy loved Mama's cake as much as Max and I did, so I knew he wasn't kidding.

I looked at Pebbles. She was just so darn cute, and I wanted to hug her so badly, but I didn't. I picked up my unicorn blanket that was draped over the gate. "Pebbles, my sweet girl, I brought you a blanket to keep you warm." I showed her the blanket and laid it down by her feet and backed away. Then I showed her Stinky. "And this is my good friend—Stinky—he always makes me feel better! I'm sure he will do the same for you." I tossed Stinky on the floor by the blanket. Before I left, I went over and got Blu and let her in Pebbles' stable. This way, Pebbles would have a friend at night in case she was scared. "Goodnight, sweet girl," I said as I blew Pebbles a kiss. I walked out of the barn with a heavy heart. I hoped one day we would be good friends.

7

A NEW DAY

The next day, I woke up feeling much better. The disappointment of how I THOUGHT my first meeting with Pebbles would go had started to subside. My mind was clearer and I decided that I would NOT give up on my pony. I quickly got dressed—I even remembered to brush my teeth—and ran downstairs, passing Mama in the kitchen on my way to the barn. Max was already up, helping Daddy collect eggs from the chicken coop. I ran past them yelling, "Morning, Daddy, morning, twerp!"

I felt like I couldn't get to the stable fast enough to see my pony. I was filled with excitement and hope. Maybe today would be the day that Pebbles and I became friends! When I reached the barn, I saw Pebbles and Blu snuggled up together in her stable. Pebbles was on the unicorn blanket I had left for her. Seeing her sleeping peacefully on MY blanket, made my heart happy. Then I noticed that Stinky was there too, under Pebbles. I knew Stinky would make her feel better! Smiling, I opened the gate. The smell of fresh hay hit my nose. It was a familiar smell that immediately comforted me.

I said good morning to both Pebbles and Blu. Blu jumped up and hopped out like the silly goat she was. Pebbles was slower to get up, but something had changed about her. . . I just hadn't figured out what it was, not even if it was a good or a bad change.

I let Pebbles out of her stable and then went about my morning chores. I fed Pebbles first then the other farm animals. On my way back to the barn, I noticed that Pebbles had found Blu and was back to following her around. I felt pretty confident so I went right over to Pebbles. I made sure to use a calm and soothing voice.

"Hi, sweet girl, you're such a good pony. Did you sleep well?" I asked as if my pony would answer me back. "I hope Stinky and Blu made your first night in your new home easier. You may not trust me yet, and that's okay, but I am SO happy you are here, I know we are going to be good friends." Then something wonderful happened— Pebbles didn't back away from me!

I was elated, but tried my best not to get overly excited so I wouldn't scare Pebbles. I reached a hand out, and guess

what happened? She let me pet her! Can you believe it? My pony actually let me touch her! It was a wonderful feeling—her soft mane under my fingers. Her eyes had softened toward me, like she understood that I may have been a little crazy but she was safe with me. I was so happy I could have cried. I wanted to grab her and hug her as tight as I could, but something told me that would not be a good idea. Maybe that was what was different about her today, maybe she was finally bonding with me!

I didn't dare to brush her just yet, I didn't think we were at that step of our relationship. Maybe Pebbles and I would have our own secret language like the grown-ups do with their looks. I couldn't explain it, but in that moment, I could have sworn Pebbles knew how loved she was.

I wanted to call Emma and tell her all about my amazing morning and the breakthrough Pebbles and I had just had, but I couldn't because I'd never told her about our bumpy start. I was beginning to think that NOT telling Emma everything was a mistake. Emma was my best friend; of course she would have understood why I was upset.

Mr. Buttons came into the barn with his favorite stick that he hid behind the chicken coop every night. He didn't think anyone knew his hiding spot but Max and I followed him one day and found it.

"Hiya, boy!" I said, giving Mr. Buttons a big hug. I was so happy to see someone that I could share my exciting news with. . . even if it was a slobbery old dog.

"Guess what. . . Pebbles and I are almost best friends," I told him. "Isn't that wonderful?" I threw his stick in the distance and Mr. Buttons ran off to retrieve it. Suddenly something caught my eye by the barn door. How had I missed it before? It was the birthday bag that Emma had brought over yesterday. I jumped up and ran over to open it. I read the card first: *Happy Birthday to my bestest friend in the whole wide world! In case you didn't get a unicorn for your birthday. . . I wanted you to have this! Love you, Em."* Reading the card made me miss Emma even more. I opened the bag and pulled out an adorable stuffed unicorn the size of Mr. Buttons! It was so soft and cuddly; I immediately gave it a tight squeeze. Emma knew exactly what I loved! Then I noticed something else in the bag. I reached back in and pulled out a little box with a beautiful unicorn bracelet in it. It was a best friend charm bracelet. I had half, and I guessed Emma had the other half. I had to call her and thank her for the lovely gifts.

I ran into the house and dialed Emma's number.

"Oh, hi, Lulu, how are you feeling?"

Hearing Emma's voice on the other end instantly gave me bubbles in my belly. I hadn't thought about it until this very moment, but what if Emma had seen me duck away from the window? Could she be mad at me?

"Hi, Em, I'm feeling much better, thanks," I said, forgetting for a moment about my little white lie from yesterday. "Thank you so much for the perfect birthday presents, I LOVE them both! Thank you, thank you, thank you!"

"You're welcome!" Emma replied. "Hey, I met your big birthday present. . . oh my goodness, Lulu, Pebbles is SO cute! Do you LOVE her so much? I bet she LOVES you SO much! How's everything going? I can't wait to come over and play with Pebbles."

Come over?! Oh no, if Emma comes over now, she'll know everything! I thought. *And what if Emma is overly excited when she sees Pebbles? She may scare her. Or, if Emma and I get overly excited to see each other, then we BOTH may scare Pebbles, and then all the progress I've made with her will be ruined!*

"Aww, thanks, Emma," I managed to say. "Umm. . . things are going really great! Pebbles is a really good pony; we are practically inseparable." Mama would not have been happy with me right then if she heard all those lies.

"That's so awesome, Lulu! So, can I come over to play today?" I could hear Emma's excitement through the phone.

"Oh. . . well. . . umm. . . actually, I don't think that's a good idea, Em. I have a lot of chores to do today, and it's only Pebbles' second day here so I should probably spend time with her. But we'll get together real soon, okay?" The guilt of lying to my friend made me feel terrible.

"I could just come for an hour," Emma suggested, "and we'd be with Pebbles together so you wouldn't be leaving her at all!"

Yikes! How could I respond to such a thoughtful solution? I loved the idea of my best friend and I spending time with Pebbles, like a dream! But the dream wasn't quite working because Pebbles didn't fully trust me yet, and if Emma came round Pebbles might back away again. I couldn't risk Emma getting in the way of Pebbles' and my friendship.

"No, sorry!" I said, not knowing what else to say. "Mama's calling! Got to go!" I hung up before Emma could say a word. I felt guilty though, and that feeling followed me around all day.

That was the last time I spoke to Emma in two whole weeks…

8

SOMETHING'S MISSING

"Happy two weeks of being in your new home, Pebbles!" I said as I walked into the barn. Pebbles and Blu were just waking up. The silly goat had been sleeping with Pebbles every night since that first night. Pebbles was still lying down with Stinky on the unicorn blanket I'd given her when she'd arrived. As soon as I opened the gate, Blu skedaddled.

Pebbles and I had made a lot of progress in the last two weeks! Not only had she got used to letting me get close to her, she also let me pet her!

"Good morning, sweet girl," I said. Pebbles looked like she was happy to see me and embraced her pets.

Everyday my friendship with Pebbles became stronger and she seemed to trust me a little more than the day before. She even felt comfortable enough with me to let me hug her. I still couldn't brush her just yet. . . but that was okay. . . we'd work on that.

One morning, after I'd fed Pebbles her breakfast, I went about my morning chores, and then I noticed something different, something wonderful—I wasn't alone! Pebbles had started following me around like a little puppy. THIS was exactly how I had imagined our friendship would be. My love for Pebbles had sprouted like a flower. The more she trusted me and let her guard down, the more my love grew for her. I couldn't wait to see her when I woke up in the morning, and she had become my favorite person (or pony) to talk to during the day. I would talk to Pebbles for hours, telling her everything—even my deepest, darkest secrets—like when I'd hidden that mean Kelly Coe's favorite pen in class because she said I looked weird. I didn't regret it, not one bit! She'd had it coming.

During those two weeks, Pebbles and I went from becoming friendly to being inseparable. I loved feeling her soft mane under my fingers, and her warm breath on my face as I leaned in for a kiss. She was the cutest thing ever and she was all mine. I sometimes wondered why I had ever questioned if she was the right pony. She was a perfect fit in our family. Sometimes, when Max and I would play hide-and-seek in the barn, I could have sworn that Pebbles and Blu wanted to play too; hiding in there became impossible because Pebbles would follow me around and Blu would follow her around and then my hiding spot would be ruined! It may be easy to hide a kid in a barn, but not a kid and a pony and a loud goat! Blu hung around us a lot. He was never too far from Pebbles. The two of them had become best barn friends.

One day, while we were sitting in the barn having our afternoon snack (carrots and apples for Pebbles, and apples and cookies for me since I hate carrots), a thought crossed my mind, a thought that gave me uncertain bubbles in my belly. Although my relationship with Pebbles was turning into exactly what I had hoped for, I still felt a little sadness in my heart—like something was missing. I didn't think it had anything to do with my new friendship with Pebbles. . . but it did have everything to do with my old friendship with Emma. And that's when it hit me; no matter how much I loved talking to Pebbles, it wasn't the same as talking to Emma.

I wanted to call Emma and tell her how close Pebbles and I had become, and to find out what she had been doing, but I couldn't even remember the last time I had spoken to Emma. How long had it been?

9

REUNITED

The next morning, I woke up thinking about my other best friend—not Pebbles but Emma. Thinking about Emma usually made me feel happy, but that morning I had uneasy bubbles in my belly. I tried to remember when the last time was that I had spoken to her. Ever since I'd thought about her yesterday, my heart had seemed to grow a whole lot sadder without her. *OMG—I can't believe it—it's been two whole weeks since I've spoken to Emma!* I realized. *I focused so much of my time on building a relationship with Pebbles, what if that's made me ruin my relationship with Emma?*

After I brushed my hair and teeth (I'll admit not my best effort), I ran outside to see Pebbles. I must have slept in because Daddy had already fed the animals, including Pebbles. She was already outside with Blu when I got to her. I decided I would eat my oatmeal outside, maybe because I was feeling a little lonely and needed her company. I gave her a gentle hug, and she embraced it. I wondered if she could feel the sadness in my heart.

"Pebbles, I love you so much and I'm so happy we are friends," I began, "but I don't think I've been a very good friend to Emma. I was too embarrassed for her to know that we had a rocky start, and I pushed her away.

She's been my best friend since kindergarten. You'd really like Emma. She's kind and fun and a great friend." The more I spoke, the sadder I felt. I think Pebbles could feel my sadness.

Max came running over with Mr. Buttons by his side. Mr. Buttons had his stick in his mouth. "Lulu, Daddy said to bring Pebbles into the barn. The vet is coming to give her a checkup."

Did I mention that our vet was no other than Dr. Burns, Emma's dad?! My belly started feeling nervous. What if Emma had told Dr. Burns that we hadn't spoken in two weeks? What if he was mad at me? What would I say if he asked why I hadn't spoken to Emma? I took a deep breath. I guessed this was one of those times that I had to put on my "big girl pants" and face whatever was about to happen. After all, what was most important was that Pebbles needed a checkup, and I certainly wanted to make sure she was healthy and well.

"Let's go, girl" I said, slowly getting up. We walked into the barn and greeted Daddy and Dr. Burns.

"There she is!" Daddy announced.

"Hi, Dr. Burns, hi, Daddy," I said quietly, my voice cracking.

"Hi, sweetie, I haven't seen you around recently, I bet your new pony is keeping you busy!" Dr. Burns said, smiling. There was nothing behind his statement, he was just making small talk.

"Um. . . yeah, I guess," I replied. Seeing Emma's dad made me miss my best friend even more. The sadness started bubbling up inside me again.

Pebbles stood there like a good girl as the vet started her checkup.

"How's Emma?" I finally managed to ask.

"She's good, I'm sure she misses you. I convinced her to come with me, she's waiting in the car. . ." he replied.

What. . . Emma's here??? My eyes got big.

She would normally have jumped out of the car. I suddenly felt very awkward in my own skin. Our friendship had changed, and it was all my fault. The fact that Emma had to be convinced to come along made me feel terrible. My mind was spinning with thoughts.

I knew what I had to do. I had to make things right with Emma…

10

DECISIONS

As nervous as I was to see Emma, a flutter of excitement also went through my bones. After all, I'd missed my best friend.

"Hi, Emma!" I yelled before I even reached the car.

"Oh. . . hey, Lulu. I thought you'd be busy with Pebbles so. . ." Emma said as she lowered the window, still sitting in the car.

I looked down quickly, realizing that I had been spending all my time with Pebbles. I had that coming. I didn't know what to say. Then the floodgates of my mouth opened and my feelings just poured out like warm syrup.

"Em, I'm so sorry! I know I've been a terrible friend. I've missed you so much!" The words were honest, I let down my guard, but Emma didn't say anything. "Please say something... I'm really sorry. There's a really good reason for why I've been distant, and I know I should have just been honest with you from the beginning and told you but..."

Emma cut me off before I could finish my thought. "Honest... about what? What are you talking about?" Emma looked completely confused. I could see her arms still crossed.

"Well, the truth is... Pebbles and I didn't have a good start... I mean... it wasn't what I thought it would be. The day we picked up Pebbles, she was frightened of me and I thought she didn't like me. . . and I was too embarrassed for you to know that my pony didn't fall in love with me instantly like I did with her! I'm sorry, I should have told you. But instead, I pushed you away."

Hearing this, Emma seemed to soften. Her arms unfolded and her face relaxed.

"Why didn't you just tell me? I would have understood. . . I thought we were best friends. . . we're supposed to tell each other everything!"

"You're right, I know, and I'm really, really sorry, Em. I was going to call you this morning and tell you everything, and then Max said your dad was here. . ."

Suddenly I heard the door unlock, Emma stepped out. I couldn't help myself—being so close to her—my arms flung out and I squeezed her tight.

"I missed you so much, Em, I talked about you to Pebbles."

"Really? You missed me?" Emma asked,

hugging me tight. "I thought you didn't have time for me now that you have Pebbles."

"Time for you? Of course I have time for you, you're my best friend! I know I've been spending a lot of time with Pebbles, but that's only because I've been working so hard to form a bond with her. It had absolutely nothing to do with not wanting to hang out with you," I admitted.

"Lulu, I get it. Do you remember when we got our dog, Cookie? She was a rescue and it took her weeks before she would come close to anyone in the family." I had forgotten all about Cookie.

"That's right," I said. "Thanks for understanding. You always know how to make me feel better. I promise I won't ever shut you out again, Em. I'm so sorry. Can you please stay for a while?"

Emma nodded and gave me a hug. For the first time in weeks, my heart was full of happiness. I had my two best friends!

Although I felt a sigh of relief that Emma had been so cool about forgiving me, I knew I had to make it up to her by showing her that I really meant what I said. I loved and missed her and I valued her friendship.

"C'mon, let's see if your dad is done with Pebbles' checkup."

When we got to the barn, Dr. Burns was packing up his bag. "Well, Lulu, I'm happy to report that you have a very healthy little pony here," he said with a smile.

"Thanks, Dr. Burns!" I replied.

"Daddy, can I please stay here and hang out with Lulu and Pebbles for a while?" Emma asked.

"Sure, I have some errands to run, so I'll come back and pick you up in the afternoon if that's okay?" Dr. Burns asked, turning toward Daddy.

"Of course, Emma is welcome to stay as long as she'd like," Daddy replied. Daddy and Dr. Burns exchanged one of those grown-up looks and smiled. I guessed

Dr. Burns knew the secret language too. Mr. Buttons and Daddy led Dr. Burns out of the barn. Like I said, nothing happened on the farm without Mr. Buttons being involved; he was like our very own barking security guard.

Emma approached Pebbles slowly. "Hi, girl, remember me?"

Pebbles looked unsure and moved closer to me. "It's okay, Pebbles, Emma is going to be around a lot, I told you all about her, remember?" I said, reassuring Pebbles. Emma looked at me and smiled. "I told her all about you, after all. . . you ARE my best friend."

The two-week gap in our friendship didn't seem like a lifetime anymore. The comfort of having my two best friends with me made me so happy I could have jumped right out of my overalls.

"So how is it, having your very own pony. . . for real?" Emma asked.

"It's great but it's definitely a lot of

responsibility," I said, which was the truth. We led Pebbles out of the barn. Blu spotted us and jumped right over, happy to be reunited with his barn buddy.

We spent the afternoon playing hide-and-seek with Max, and hanging out with Pebbles. I felt complete.

After lunch, we sat in the barn next to Pebbles' stable. "Are you still coming with us to the lake tomorrow?" Emma asked.

With everything going on, I had completely forgotten about the lake. Every year, Emma's family invited me to join them at their lake house in the spring. We always had the best time together and looked forward to the trip all year long.

"Of course I am, if I'm still invited. . . I didn't know if you still wanted me to come," I replied.

"Of course I want you to come, it wouldn't be the same without you," Emma insisted.

"Oh good, I can't wait," I said.

"Lulu, I was so worried that you wouldn't want to leave Pebbles. . ." Emma's words stopped my thought process in its tracks. Pebbles? Oh no, I had forgotten all about my promise to Daddy that I would always take care of Pebbles. After all, responsibility doesn't take a day off, you know! How could I take care of Pebbles if I wasn't here? And how could I possibly think about leaving now when we were just starting to bond?! If I left her, would she feel abandoned? Would it ruin the trust we had just built? But if I didn't go, Emma would be upset and think I was choosing Pebbles over her again. I had to prove to Emma that our friendship was just as important.

"The thing is. . . I haven't even thought about leaving Pebbles, I've been so busy with her. . . I forgot all about the trip."

"It's okay," Emma said, "you have had a lot of things going on."

"I really want to come with you," I said, deciding to be honest. "But I'm worried about leaving Pebbles."

"I understand that. I hope you will still come," Emma said slowly.

"I'm sure I can," I said, although I sounded more like I was trying to convince myself than her. The bubbles were back in my belly. They weren't as big as before and I knew that was because I had done something very responsible—I had been honest with Emma, and that felt good. But they were still there because I just didn't know what to do!

11

BALANCE

That night it took me a long time to fall asleep. The bubbles kept bubbling and popping in my belly. I couldn't stop thinking of my conundrum! What was I going to do? I didn't want Mama and Daddy to think I wasn't responsible, and I was worried about leaving Pebbles when we were just starting to bond. But I also didn't want to disappoint Emma. I felt like the weight of the world was on my shoulders. And to make matters worse, I could hear that little twerp fast asleep snoring, probably dreaming of chasing Mr. Buttons around the farm.

My eyes felt very heavy that morning when Mama came in to wake me up. I was so tired that my brain hurt, probably from all the thinking I had done last night. After I brushed my teeth, I went downstairs for breakfast.

"Good morning, sunshine," Daddy said with a big smile.

Max and Mama were already eating. Max was stuffing his face with Mama's delicious pancakes. I don't think he even knew I was there.

"Hi," was all I could manage to say.

"Lulu, honey, are you okay? You look like you have something on your mind." Mama was always quick to know when something was up.

"Well. . ." I began, not knowing what was going to come out of my mouth next. "The thing is. . . Emma's lake trip is today and. . ."

"That's right, you girls always have such a great time!" Mama interrupted before I could finish my sentence.

"Well. . . that's just it, I would like to go but. . ."

"But? What's the but about?" Daddy asked.

Then the unexpected happened, before I could say a word, uncontrollable tears started down my face.

"Lulu, baby, what's wrong?" Mama asked, totally confused.

"Why is Lulu crying?" The little twerp now noticed I was in the room.

"I. . . I. . . I don't want to disappoint anyone!" I finally blurted out.

"What on earth are you talking about, honey?" Daddy asked.

"I want to go to Emma's lake house

but I don't want to leave Pebbles. And, if I go, you and Mama will think I am not responsible, and Pebbles may forget all the bonding we've done. But if I don't go, I'll disappoint Emma because she will think I chose Pebbles over her. No matter what I do, I will be disappointing someone!"

It felt good to get it all off my chest, but that didn't stop my tears from streaming. Mama came over and gave me one of her magical Mama hugs—it worked; the tears stopped immediately.

"Oh, honey," Daddy said, "we know you are responsible. You've been doing a great job taking care of Pebbles. That doesn't mean you can't go away for a weekend and have fun with your friend. You just need to make sure that someone else can take care of your responsibilities while you're away. Your mama and I will be happy to take care of Pebbles while you are gone."

"But Pebbles will miss me," I responded.

"I'm sure Pebbles will miss you, but she

has Max and Blu and Mr. Buttons, she'll be just fine. Besides, it's only a few days." Mama always knew the right thing to say. "And," she continued, "you haven't been spending a lot of time with Emma since we brought Pebbles home. It's good to be responsible. . . but it's also important to have balance."

Mama was right, it was only a few days, and Pebbles still had lots of company. She would be fine for a few days without me. And I did need balance in my life; going to the lake was maybe the only thing that could balance me! With this new revelation, I started feeling better. I realized the bubbles in belly must have been guilt bubbles because they were all starting to pop and go away. I gave Mama and Daddy a big hug and thanked them for taking care of Pebbles for me and for making me feel better. I ran upstairs to pack a bag and call Emma to tell her the good news.

After I finished my morning chores—

feeding the animals and cleaning their pens—I walked Pebbles back into the barn.

"Hi, pretty girl!" I started. My heart was a little sad. I picked up her brush (which I had never used) and instinctively started brushing her beautiful mane. She seemed to enjoy it. In that moment, I felt that our bond was strong enough to handle anything. I felt her soft hair under the brush. With my other hand I petted her long, overgrown mane. It felt wonderful to take care of her. I couldn't help but wonder if she felt just as loved in that moment?

"I have something to tell you, Pebbles," I said in my bravest voice. "I'm going to go away for a few days, but I promise I'll be back. And don't worry—you have plenty of friends here to play with, and Mama and Daddy will take good care of you while I'm gone." I had built up the courage after all these weeks to lean in and give Pebbles a big hug. As I held onto her and thought about how much I'd miss her, my heart started to

feel a little sad. . . until that silly little goat came hopping over. As soon as Pebbles saw Blu, she followed him out of the barn. And, just like that, I felt better knowing Pebbles would be just fine.

I heard Emma's car pull up and I felt a sense of excitement crawl up my back. As we drove away, I waved goodbye to our little farm. My heart was full of warmth and happiness knowing when I came back, my little pony would be there waiting for me. I blew Pebbles an extra kiss from the window.

12

BOND

The weekend at the lake flew by! Emma and I enjoyed every moment of it. We did so many things; swimming in the lake, fishing, tubing and just hanging out. Mama was right, having balance in your life was important. Even though I had my responsibilities at home, I could still have fun and enjoy being away with my best friend. I felt totally relaxed, I knew that Pebbles would be fine and well taken care of while I was gone. I went back home feeling refreshed!

By the time we returned to the farm, I was ready to see my pony. Mr. Buttons was the first one to welcome me home. He must have heard the car approaching because he tackled me halfway up the driveway, smelling me suspiciously. I don't think he liked all the lake smells I'd brought back with me, but after a few seconds, he decided I was okay, and slobbered me with wet kisses. I had to admit, I was happy to see him too. . . slobber and all.

"Hiya, boy," I said. "Did you take good care of the farm while I was gone?" I gave him a quick belly rub.

Before I said goodbye to Emma, I had one last thing to ask her, which had been on my mind since my birthday.

"Em, you know when you came to the house on my birthday and I said I was sick. . .?" I started.

"Yeah. . ." Emma gave a smile. "But you weren't really sick."

"Yep, that, did Pebbles like you?"

"What do you mean?"

"Did she back away from you? Or did she let you touch her when you went near her?" I asked. I held my breath, waiting for my best friend's answer.

"Oh, I don't know, I didn't go close. I was going to, but your dad said it was best to not touch her just yet because she was a little nervous," Emma explained.

I realized how silly I'd been to have worried about it, to have felt jealous of Emma and Pebbles. I was glad I had such a good, understanding best friend like Emma. We gave each other a hug, I thanked her parents, and then turned toward the farm. I was home.

As I made my way to the barn, I felt a little nervous. *What if Pebbles has forgotten me?* I worried, but boy was that far from the

truth!

The second Pebbles saw me, she galloped over (as much as her stubby little legs could gallop) to say hello. Her eyes looked happy in a way I had never seen before. I could tell she had missed me just as much as I'd missed her. She nuzzled up close as if she wanted a hug. As I wrapped my arms around her, my heart filled with happiness.

"Hi, sweet girl, I missed you so much! I love you, Pebbles," I said, giving her as many kisses as she would allow. That was the moment I had imagined my pony and I would have had on our first meeting. It hadn't happened that day, but I sure was happy to have that moment at last. It may have taken some time to get there, but Pebbles and I had finally built a trust, a bond and a friendship that couldn't be broken.

Max came running into the barn. "Lulu, you're back!"

I gave the little twerp a hug because I

could only imagine how terribly he must have missed me. "Hey, Max, did you take good care of Pebbles while I was away?" I asked.

Max nodded. "Daddy and I took good care of Pebbles!"

"Good boy, thanks, Max! That is very responsible of you," I replied.

"I WAS very responsible," Max agreed proudly. "In fact, Daddy said because I was so responsible, they're getting me a BIG surprise for my birthday next month. . ."